DreDreaming "What Do You See?"

by

Joneshia Cranford-Shepherd

To order additional copies of this book, contact:
Xlibris
844-714-8691
www.Xlibris.com
Orders@Xlibris.com

ISBN: 978-1-6641-3466-9 (sc)
ISBN: 978-1-6641-3465-2 (e)

Print information available on the last page

Rev. date: 10/05/2020

Book Dedication

   To my greatest gifts from God, Armanei' E'Lyse & Michael Joseph. I dedicate this book, the first of many to the both of you. I am honored that God chose me to be your Mother. I love you today even more than I did on yesterday! You two are my biggest critics, yet my greatest motivators. Thank you my sweet babies for giving me that extra push!

Love,
Mama

Hello! My name is Andre'! My family and close friends call me "Dre" for short. I'm just your average boy who likes to play outside and try new things.

Can I share something with you that makes me feel a little weird sometimes? Some people take one look at my mocha brown skin and form judgements about me.

What do you see when you look at me?
Do you see my expensive sneakers?

SCHOOL REPORT CARD

SUBJECT	1st Qtr.	2nd Qtr
MATH	F	B
ART	F	B

My parents surprised me with them for bringing my Math and Art grades up to a B. I had to work hard for good grades. It felt good to make them proud.

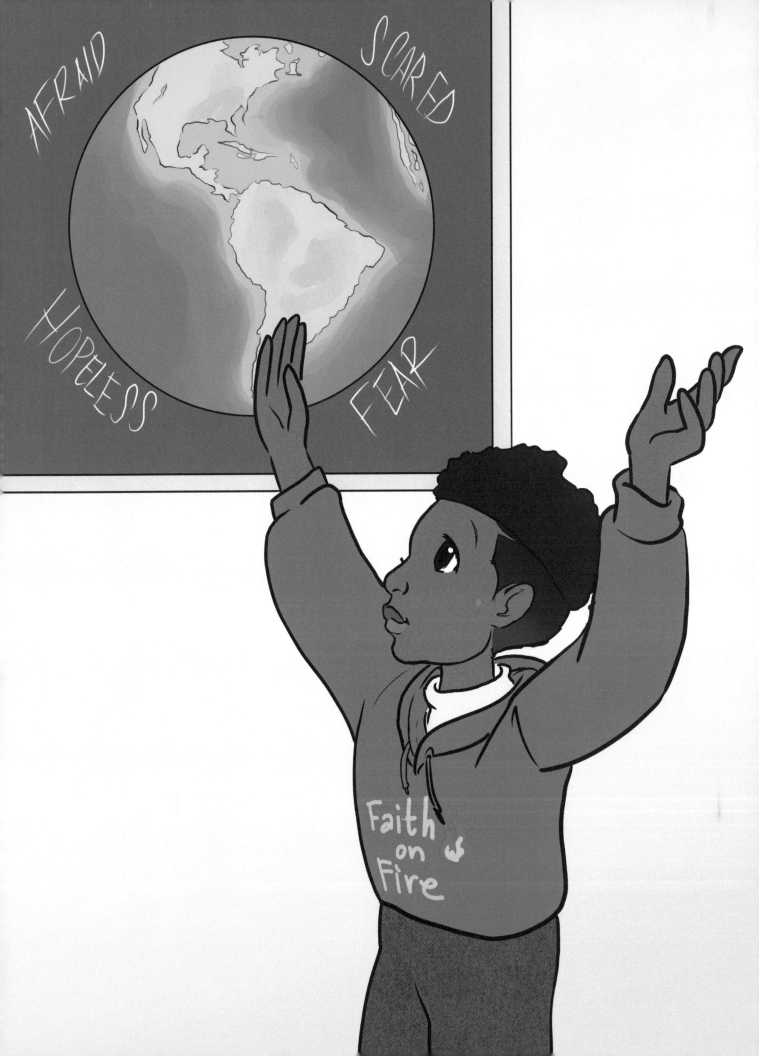

Do you see my favorite blue hoodie? It keeps me warm and makes me feel SECURE in a world full of INSECURITY.

Do you see my hands in my pockets? I keep them there for confidence. It reminds me to look people in the eye when we are speaking to one another.

Do you see my strong arms and big hands? Me? Play football? I prefer not to tackle anyone. I want to use my strong arms and big hands to perform brain surgeries. I want to give people another chance at life.

Do you see this gold chain around my neck? It was given to me when I accepted Christ into my life. When I look at it, I remember that he died so that I can live.

Do you see my neat haircut? My barber is the best! He creates a new hair design for me each week. I get so excited when my dad takes me to the barbershop.

Do you see the squint of my eyes and frown on my face? Angry? Of course not, but my mother would be if she knew I forgot to wear my glasses. SHHHHHHHHH!!!!!!!!! Please, don't tell her.

Do you see my rather large shorts? No, I'm not sagging. My dad buys my shorts a size bigger so that I can grow into them. He said that I am "growing like a weed", whatever that means.

Did you see these things when you looked at me? Did my mocha brown skin and outer appearance tell you something different about me?

Please get to know me inside before you judge me from the outside. I am so much more. I am more than my mocha brown skin, more than my shoes, more than my hoodie, more than my hands in my pocket, more than football, more than my gold chain, more than my hair, more than my shoes, and more than my facial expressions.

I am simply a boy who goes by the name "Dre", dreaming of my bright future ahead.

Meet Ann Loughton-
Dre's Mother

Meet Ark Loughton-
Dre's Father